HOUSE SITTING GUIDE F

MW00961331

VET INFORMATION

NAME: PHONE:

ADDRESS:

ROUTE:

NAME AND AGE:

BREED:

MEALTIMES:

FOOD AND WATER:

TREATS:

FAVORITE TOYS:

NOTES AND INSTRUCTIONS

NAME AND AGE:

BREED:

MEALTIMES:

FOOD AND WATER:

TREATS:

FAVORITE TOYS:

NOTES AND INSTRUCTIONS

NAME AND AGE:

BREED:

MEALTIMES:

FOOD AND WATER:

TREATS:

FAVORITE TOYS:

NOTES AND INSTRUCTIONS

NAME AND AGE:

BREED:

MEALTIMES:

FOOD AND WATER:

TREATS:

FAVORITE TOYS:

NOTES AND INSTRUCTIONS

HOUSE SITTING GUIDE PET INFORMATION

VET INFORMATION	
NAME:	PHONE:
ADDRESS:	
ROUTE:	

NAME AND AGE:
BREED:
MEALTIMES:
FOOD AND WATER:
TREATS:
FAVORITE TOYS:
NOTES AND INSTRUCTIONS

NAME AND AGE:
BREED:
MEALTIMES:
FOOD AND WATER:
TREATS:
FAVORITE TOYS:
NOTES AND INSTRUCTIONS

NAME AND AGE:
BREED:
MEALTIMES:
FOOD AND WATER:
TREATS:
FAVORITE TOYS:
NOTES AND INSTRUCTIONS

NAME AND AGE:
BREED:
MEALTIMES:
FOOD AND WATER:
TREATS:
FAVORITE TOYS:
NOTES AND INSTRUCTIONS

HOUSE SITTING GUIDE PET INFORMATION

VET INFORMATION	
NAME:	PHONE:
ADDRESS:	
ROUTE:	

NAME AND AGE:
BREED:
MEALTIMES:
FOOD AND WATER:
TREATS:
FAVORITE TOYS:
NOTES AND INSTRUCTIONS

NAME AND AGE:
BREED:
MEALTIMES:
FOOD AND WATER:
TREATS:
FAVORITE TOYS:
NOTES AND INSTRUCTIONS

NAME AND AGE:
BREED:
MEALTIMES:
FOOD AND WATER:
TREATS:
FAVORITE TOYS:
NOTES AND INSTRUCTIONS

NAME AND AGE:
BREED:
MEALTIMES:
FOOD AND WATER:
TREATS:
FAVORITE TOYS:
NOTES AND INSTRUCTIONS

HOUSE SITTING GUIDE PET INFORMATION

VET INFORMATION	
NAME:	PHONE:
ADDRESS:	
ROUTE:	

NAME AND AGE:
BREED:
MEALTIMES:
FOOD AND WATER:
TREATS:
FAVORITE TOYS:
NOTES AND INSTRUCTIONS

NAME AND AGE:
BREED:
MEALTIMES:
FOOD AND WATER:
TREATS:
FAVORITE TOYS:
NOTES AND INSTRUCTIONS

NAME AND AGE:
BREED:
MEALTIMES:
FOOD AND WATER:
TREATS:
FAVORITE TOYS:
NOTES AND INSTRUCTIONS

NAME AND AGE:
BREED:
MEALTIMES:
FOOD AND WATER:
TREATS:
FAVORITE TOYS:
NOTES AND INSTRUCTIONS

HOUSE SITTING GUIDE PET INFORMATION

VET INFORMATION

NAME: PHONE:

ADDRESS:

ROUTE:

NAME AND AGE:

BREED:

MEALTIMES:

FOOD AND WATER:

TREATS:

FAVORITE TOYS:

NOTES AND INSTRUCTIONS

NAME AND AGE:

BREED:

MEALTIMES:

FOOD AND WATER:

TREATS:

FAVORITE TOYS:

NOTES AND INSTRUCTIONS

NAME AND AGE:

BREED:

MEALTIMES:

FOOD AND WATER:

TREATS:

FAVORITE TOYS:

NOTES AND INSTRUCTIONS

NAME AND AGE:

BREED:

MEALTIMES:

FOOD AND WATER:

TREATS:

FAVORITE TOYS:

NOTES AND INSTRUCTIONS

HOUSE SITTING GUIDE PET INFORMATION

VET INFORMATION	
NAME:	PHONE:
ADDRESS:	
ROUTE:	

NAME AND AGE:
BREED:
MEALTIMES:
FOOD AND WATER:
TREATS:
FAVORITE TOYS:
NOTES AND INSTRUCTIONS

NAME AND AGE:
BREED:
MEALTIMES:
FOOD AND WATER:
TREATS:
FAVORITE TOYS:
NOTES AND INSTRUCTIONS

NAME AND AGE:
BREED:
MEALTIMES:
FOOD AND WATER:
TREATS:
FAVORITE TOYS:
NOTES AND INSTRUCTIONS

NAME AND AGE:
BREED:
MEALTIMES:
FOOD AND WATER:
TREATS:
FAVORITE TOYS:
NOTES AND INSTRUCTIONS

HOUSE SITTING GUIDE PET INFORMATION

VET INFORMATION

NAME: PHONE:

ADDRESS:

ROUTE:

NAME AND AGE:

BREED:

MEALTIMES:

FOOD AND WATER:

TREATS:

FAVORITE TOYS:

NOTES AND INSTRUCTIONS

NAME AND AGE:

BREED:

MEALTIMES:

FOOD AND WATER:

TREATS:

FAVORITE TOYS:

NOTES AND INSTRUCTIONS

NAME AND AGE:

BREED:

MEALTIMES:

FOOD AND WATER:

TREATS:

FAVORITE TOYS:

NOTES AND INSTRUCTIONS

NAME AND AGE:

BREED:

MEALTIMES:

FOOD AND WATER:

TREATS:

FAVORITE TOYS:

NOTES AND INSTRUCTIONS

HOUSE SITTING GUIDE PET INFORMATION

VET INFORMATION	
NAME:	PHONE:
ADDRESS:	
ROUTE:	

NAME AND AGE:
BREED:
MEALTIMES:
FOOD AND WATER:
TREATS:
FAVORITE TOYS:
NOTES AND INSTRUCTIONS

NAME AND AGE:
BREED:
MEALTIMES:
FOOD AND WATER:
TREATS:
FAVORITE TOYS:
NOTES AND INSTRUCTIONS

NAME AND AGE:
BREED:
MEALTIMES:
FOOD AND WATER:
TREATS:
FAVORITE TOYS:
NOTES AND INSTRUCTIONS

NAME AND AGE:
BREED:
MEALTIMES:
FOOD AND WATER:
TREATS:
FAVORITE TOYS:
NOTES AND INSTRUCTIONS

HOUSE SITTING GUIDE PET INFORMATION

VET INFORMATION	
NAME:	PHONE:
ADDRESS:	
ROUTE:	

NAME AND AGE:
BREED:
MEALTIMES:
FOOD AND WATER:
TREATS:
FAVORITE TOYS:
NOTES AND INSTRUCTIONS

NAME AND AGE:
BREED:
MEALTIMES:
FOOD AND WATER:
TREATS:
FAVORITE TOYS:
NOTES AND INSTRUCTIONS

NAME AND AGE:
BREED:
MEALTIMES:
FOOD AND WATER:
TREATS:
FAVORITE TOYS:
NOTES AND INSTRUCTIONS

NAME AND AGE:
BREED:
MEALTIMES:
FOOD AND WATER:
TREATS:
FAVORITE TOYS:
NOTES AND INSTRUCTIONS

HOUSE SITTING GUIDE PET INFORMATION

VET INFORMATION

NAME: PHONE:

ADDRESS:

ROUTE:

NAME AND AGE:

BREED:

MEALTIMES:

FOOD AND WATER:

TREATS:

FAVORITE TOYS:

NOTES AND INSTRUCTIONS

NAME AND AGE:

BREED:

MEALTIMES:

FOOD AND WATER:

TREATS:

FAVORITE TOYS:

NOTES AND INSTRUCTIONS

NAME AND AGE:

BREED:

MEALTIMES:

FOOD AND WATER:

TREATS:

FAVORITE TOYS:

NOTES AND INSTRUCTIONS

NAME AND AGE:

BREED:

MEALTIMES:

FOOD AND WATER:

TREATS:

FAVORITE TOYS:

NOTES AND INSTRUCTIONS

HOUSE SITTING GUIDE PET INFORMATION

VET INFORMATION

NAME: PHONE:

ADDRESS:

ROUTE:

NAME AND AGE:

BREED:

MEALTIMES:

FOOD AND WATER:

TREATS:

FAVORITE TOYS:

NOTES AND INSTRUCTIONS

NAME AND AGE:

BREED:

MEALTIMES:

FOOD AND WATER:

TREATS:

FAVORITE TOYS:

NOTES AND INSTRUCTIONS

NAME AND AGE:

BREED:

MEALTIMES:

FOOD AND WATER:

TREATS:

FAVORITE TOYS:

NOTES AND INSTRUCTIONS

NAME AND AGE:

BREED:

MEALTIMES:

FOOD AND WATER:

TREATS:

FAVORITE TOYS:

NOTES AND INSTRUCTIONS

HOUSE SITTING GUIDE PET INFORMATION

VET INFORMATION	
NAME:	PHONE:
ADDRESS:	
ROUTE:	

NAME AND AGE:
BREED:
MEALTIMES:
FOOD AND WATER:
TREATS:
FAVORITE TOYS:
NOTES AND INSTRUCTIONS

NAME AND AGE:
BREED:
MEALTIMES:
FOOD AND WATER:
TREATS:
FAVORITE TOYS:
NOTES AND INSTRUCTIONS

NAME AND AGE:
BREED:
MEALTIMES:
FOOD AND WATER:
TREATS:
FAVORITE TOYS:
NOTES AND INSTRUCTIONS

NAME AND AGE:
BREED:
MEALTIMES:
FOOD AND WATER:
TREATS:
FAVORITE TOYS:
NOTES AND INSTRUCTIONS

HOUSE SITTING GUIDE PET INFORMATION

VET INFORMATION	
NAME:	PHONE:
ADDRESS:	
ROUTE:	

NAME AND AGE:
BREED:
MEALTIMES:
FOOD AND WATER:
TREATS:
FAVORITE TOYS:
NOTES AND INSTRUCTIONS

NAME AND AGE:
BREED:
MEALTIMES:
FOOD AND WATER:
TREATS:
FAVORITE TOYS:
NOTES AND INSTRUCTIONS

NAME AND AGE:
BREED:
MEALTIMES:
FOOD AND WATER:
TREATS:
FAVORITE TOYS:
NOTES AND INSTRUCTIONS

NAME AND AGE:
BREED:
MEALTIMES:
FOOD AND WATER:
TREATS:
FAVORITE TOYS:
NOTES AND INSTRUCTIONS

HOUSE SITTING GUIDE PET INFORMATION

VET INFORMATION

NAME: PHONE:

ADDRESS:

ROUTE:

NAME AND AGE:

BREED:

MEALTIMES:

FOOD AND WATER:

TREATS:

FAVORITE TOYS:

NOTES AND INSTRUCTIONS

NAME AND AGE:

BREED:

MEALTIMES:

FOOD AND WATER:

TREATS:

FAVORITE TOYS:

NOTES AND INSTRUCTIONS

NAME AND AGE:

BREED:

MEALTIMES:

FOOD AND WATER:

TREATS:

FAVORITE TOYS:

NOTES AND INSTRUCTIONS

NAME AND AGE:

BREED:

MEALTIMES:

FOOD AND WATER:

TREATS:

FAVORITE TOYS:

NOTES AND INSTRUCTIONS

HOUSE SITTING GUIDE PET INFORMATION

VET INFORMATION

NAME: PHONE:

ADDRESS:

ROUTE:

NAME AND AGE:

BREED:

MEALTIMES:

FOOD AND WATER:

TREATS:

FAVORITE TOYS:

NOTES AND INSTRUCTIONS

NAME AND AGE:

BREED:

MEALTIMES:

FOOD AND WATER:

TREATS:

FAVORITE TOYS:

NOTES AND INSTRUCTIONS

NAME AND AGE:

BREED:

MEALTIMES:

FOOD AND WATER:

TREATS:

FAVORITE TOYS:

NOTES AND INSTRUCTIONS

NAME AND AGE:

BREED:

MEALTIMES:

FOOD AND WATER:

TREATS:

FAVORITE TOYS:

NOTES AND INSTRUCTIONS

HOUSE SITTING GUIDE PET INFORMATION

VET INFORMATION	
NAME:	PHONE:
ADDRESS:	
ROUTE:	

NAME AND AGE:
BREED:
MEALTIMES:
FOOD AND WATER:
TREATS:
FAVORITE TOYS:
NOTES AND INSTRUCTIONS

NAME AND AGE:
BREED:
MEALTIMES:
FOOD AND WATER:
TREATS:
FAVORITE TOYS:
NOTES AND INSTRUCTIONS

NAME AND AGE:
BREED:
MEALTIMES:
FOOD AND WATER:
TREATS:
FAVORITE TOYS:
NOTES AND INSTRUCTIONS

NAME AND AGE:
BREED:
MEALTIMES:
FOOD AND WATER:
TREATS:
FAVORITE TOYS:
NOTES AND INSTRUCTIONS

HOUSE SITTING GUIDE PET INFORMATION

VET INFORMATION	
NAME:	PHONE:
ADDRESS:	
ROUTE:	

NAME AND AGE:
BREED:
MEALTIMES:
FOOD AND WATER:
TREATS:
FAVORITE TOYS:
NOTES AND INSTRUCTIONS

NAME AND AGE:
BREED:
MEALTIMES:
FOOD AND WATER:
TREATS:
FAVORITE TOYS:
NOTES AND INSTRUCTIONS

NAME AND AGE:
BREED:
MEALTIMES:
FOOD AND WATER:
TREATS:
FAVORITE TOYS:
NOTES AND INSTRUCTIONS

NAME AND AGE:
BREED:
MEALTIMES:
FOOD AND WATER:
TREATS:
FAVORITE TOYS:
NOTES AND INSTRUCTIONS

HOUSE SITTING GUIDE PET INFORMATION

VET INFORMATION

NAME: PHONE:

ADDRESS:

ROUTE:

NAME AND AGE:

BREED:

MEALTIMES:

FOOD AND WATER:

TREATS:

FAVORITE TOYS:

NOTES AND INSTRUCTIONS

NAME AND AGE:

BREED:

MEALTIMES:

FOOD AND WATER:

TREATS:

FAVORITE TOYS:

NOTES AND INSTRUCTIONS

NAME AND AGE:

BREED:

MEALTIMES:

FOOD AND WATER:

TREATS:

FAVORITE TOYS:

NOTES AND INSTRUCTIONS

NAME AND AGE:

BREED:

MEALTIMES:

FOOD AND WATER:

TREATS:

FAVORITE TOYS:

NOTES AND INSTRUCTIONS

HOUSE SITTING GUIDE PET INFORMATION

VET INFORMATION

NAME:	PHONE:
ADDRESS:	
ROUTE:	

NAME AND AGE:

BREED:

MEALTIMES:

FOOD AND WATER:

TREATS:

FAVORITE TOYS:

NOTES AND INSTRUCTIONS

NAME AND AGE:

BREED:

MEALTIMES:

FOOD AND WATER:

TREATS:

FAVORITE TOYS:

NOTES AND INSTRUCTIONS

NAME AND AGE:

BREED:

MEALTIMES:

FOOD AND WATER:

TREATS:

FAVORITE TOYS:

NOTES AND INSTRUCTIONS

NAME AND AGE:

BREED:

MEALTIMES:

FOOD AND WATER:

TREATS:

FAVORITE TOYS:

NOTES AND INSTRUCTIONS

HOUSE SITTING GUIDE PET INFORMATION

VET INFORMATION

NAME: PHONE:

ADDRESS:

ROUTE:

NAME AND AGE:

BREED:

MEALTIMES:

FOOD AND WATER:

TREATS:

FAVORITE TOYS:

NOTES AND INSTRUCTIONS

NAME AND AGE:

BREED:

MEALTIMES:

FOOD AND WATER:

TREATS:

FAVORITE TOYS:

NOTES AND INSTRUCTIONS

NAME AND AGE:

BREED:

MEALTIMES:

FOOD AND WATER:

TREATS:

FAVORITE TOYS:

NOTES AND INSTRUCTIONS

NAME AND AGE:

BREED:

MEALTIMES:

FOOD AND WATER:

TREATS:

FAVORITE TOYS:

NOTES AND INSTRUCTIONS

HOUSE SITTING GUIDE PET INFORMATION

VET INFORMATION

NAME: PHONE:

ADDRESS:

ROUTE:

NAME AND AGE:

BREED:

MEALTIMES:

FOOD AND WATER:

TREATS:

FAVORITE TOYS:

NOTES AND INSTRUCTIONS

NAME AND AGE:

BREED:

MEALTIMES:

FOOD AND WATER:

TREATS:

FAVORITE TOYS:

NOTES AND INSTRUCTIONS

NAME AND AGE:

BREED:

MEALTIMES:

FOOD AND WATER:

TREATS:

FAVORITE TOYS:

NOTES AND INSTRUCTIONS

NAME AND AGE:

BREED:

MEALTIMES:

FOOD AND WATER:

TREATS:

FAVORITE TOYS:

NOTES AND INSTRUCTIONS

HOUSE SITTING GUIDE PET INFORMATION

VET INFORMATION

NAME: PHONE:

ADDRESS:

ROUTE:

NAME AND AGE:

BREED:

MEALTIMES:

FOOD AND WATER:

TREATS:

FAVORITE TOYS:

NOTES AND INSTRUCTIONS

NAME AND AGE:

BREED:

MEALTIMES:

FOOD AND WATER:

TREATS:

FAVORITE TOYS:

NOTES AND INSTRUCTIONS

NAME AND AGE:

BREED:

MEALTIMES:

FOOD AND WATER:

TREATS:

FAVORITE TOYS:

NOTES AND INSTRUCTIONS

NAME AND AGE:

BREED:

MEALTIMES:

FOOD AND WATER:

TREATS:

FAVORITE TOYS:

NOTES AND INSTRUCTIONS

HOUSE SITTING GUIDE PET INFORMATION

VET INFORMATION

NAME: PHONE:

ADDRESS:

ROUTE:

NAME AND AGE:

BREED:

MEALTIMES:

FOOD AND WATER:

TREATS:

FAVORITE TOYS:

NOTES AND INSTRUCTIONS

NAME AND AGE:

BREED:

MEALTIMES:

FOOD AND WATER:

TREATS:

FAVORITE TOYS:

NOTES AND INSTRUCTIONS

NAME AND AGE:

BREED:

MEALTIMES:

FOOD AND WATER:

TREATS:

FAVORITE TOYS:

NOTES AND INSTRUCTIONS

NAME AND AGE:

BREED:

MEALTIMES:

FOOD AND WATER:

TREATS:

FAVORITE TOYS:

NOTES AND INSTRUCTIONS

HOUSE SITTING GUIDE PET INFORMATION

VET INFORMATION

NAME: PHONE:

ADDRESS:

ROUTE:

NAME AND AGE:

BREED:

MEALTIMES:

FOOD AND WATER:

TREATS:

FAVORITE TOYS:

NOTES AND INSTRUCTIONS

NAME AND AGE:

BREED:

MEALTIMES:

FOOD AND WATER:

TREATS:

FAVORITE TOYS:

NOTES AND INSTRUCTIONS

NAME AND AGE:

BREED:

MEALTIMES:

FOOD AND WATER:

TREATS:

FAVORITE TOYS:

NOTES AND INSTRUCTIONS

NAME AND AGE:

BREED:

MEALTIMES:

FOOD AND WATER:

TREATS:

FAVORITE TOYS:

NOTES AND INSTRUCTIONS

HOUSE SITTING GUIDE PET INFORMATION

VET INFORMATION

NAME: PHONE:

ADDRESS:

ROUTE:

NAME AND AGE:

BREED:

MEALTIMES:

FOOD AND WATER:

TREATS:

FAVORITE TOYS:

NOTES AND INSTRUCTIONS

NAME AND AGE:

BREED:

MEALTIMES:

FOOD AND WATER:

TREATS:

FAVORITE TOYS:

NOTES AND INSTRUCTIONS

NAME AND AGE:

BREED:

MEALTIMES:

FOOD AND WATER:

TREATS:

FAVORITE TOYS:

NOTES AND INSTRUCTIONS

NAME AND AGE:

BREED:

MEALTIMES:

FOOD AND WATER:

TREATS:

FAVORITE TOYS:

NOTES AND INSTRUCTIONS

HOUSE SITTING GUIDE PET INFORMATION

VET INFORMATION

NAME: PHONE:

ADDRESS:

ROUTE:

NAME AND AGE:

BREED:

MEALTIMES:

FOOD AND WATER:

TREATS:

FAVORITE TOYS:

NOTES AND INSTRUCTIONS

NAME AND AGE:

BREED:

MEALTIMES:

FOOD AND WATER:

TREATS:

FAVORITE TOYS:

NOTES AND INSTRUCTIONS

NAME AND AGE:

BREED:

MEALTIMES:

FOOD AND WATER:

TREATS:

FAVORITE TOYS:

NOTES AND INSTRUCTIONS

NAME AND AGE:

BREED:

MEALTIMES:

FOOD AND WATER:

TREATS:

FAVORITE TOYS:

NOTES AND INSTRUCTIONS

HOUSE SITTING GUIDE PET INFORMATION

VET INFORMATION

NAME: PHONE:

ADDRESS:

ROUTE:

NAME AND AGE:

BREED:

MEALTIMES:

FOOD AND WATER:

TREATS:

FAVORITE TOYS:

NOTES AND INSTRUCTIONS

NAME AND AGE:

BREED:

MEALTIMES:

FOOD AND WATER:

TREATS:

FAVORITE TOYS:

NOTES AND INSTRUCTIONS

NAME AND AGE:

BREED:

MEALTIMES:

FOOD AND WATER:

TREATS:

FAVORITE TOYS:

NOTES AND INSTRUCTIONS

NAME AND AGE:

BREED:

MEALTIMES:

FOOD AND WATER:

TREATS:

FAVORITE TOYS:

NOTES AND INSTRUCTIONS

HOUSE SITTING GUIDE PET INFORMATION

VET INFORMATION

NAME: PHONE:

ADDRESS:

ROUTE:

NAME AND AGE:

BREED:

MEALTIMES:

FOOD AND WATER:

TREATS:

FAVORITE TOYS:

NOTES AND INSTRUCTIONS

NAME AND AGE:

BREED:

MEALTIMES:

FOOD AND WATER:

TREATS:

FAVORITE TOYS:

NOTES AND INSTRUCTIONS

NAME AND AGE:

BREED:

MEALTIMES:

FOOD AND WATER:

TREATS:

FAVORITE TOYS:

NOTES AND INSTRUCTIONS

NAME AND AGE:

BREED:

MEALTIMES:

FOOD AND WATER:

TREATS:

FAVORITE TOYS:

NOTES AND INSTRUCTIONS

HOUSE SITTING GUIDE PET INFORMATION

VET INFORMATION

NAME: PHONE:

ADDRESS:

ROUTE:

NAME AND AGE:

BREED:

MEALTIMES:

FOOD AND WATER:

TREATS:

FAVORITE TOYS:

NOTES AND INSTRUCTIONS

NAME AND AGE:

BREED:

MEALTIMES:

FOOD AND WATER:

TREATS:

FAVORITE TOYS:

NOTES AND INSTRUCTIONS

NAME AND AGE:

BREED:

MEALTIMES:

FOOD AND WATER:

TREATS:

FAVORITE TOYS:

NOTES AND INSTRUCTIONS

NAME AND AGE:

BREED:

MEALTIMES:

FOOD AND WATER:

TREATS:

FAVORITE TOYS:

NOTES AND INSTRUCTIONS

HOUSE SITTING GUIDE PET INFORMATION

VET INFORMATION	
NAME:	PHONE:
ADDRESS:	
ROUTE:	

NAME AND AGE:

BREED:

MEALTIMES:

FOOD AND WATER:

TREATS:

FAVORITE TOYS:

NOTES AND INSTRUCTIONS

NAME AND AGE:

BREED:

MEALTIMES:

FOOD AND WATER:

TREATS:

FAVORITE TOYS:

NOTES AND INSTRUCTIONS

NAME AND AGE:

BREED:

MEALTIMES:

FOOD AND WATER:

TREATS:

FAVORITE TOYS:

NOTES AND INSTRUCTIONS

NAME AND AGE:

BREED:

MEALTIMES:

FOOD AND WATER:

TREATS:

FAVORITE TOYS:

NOTES AND INSTRUCTIONS

HOUSE SITTING GUIDE PET INFORMATION

VET INFORMATION

NAME: PHONE:

ADDRESS:

ROUTE:

NAME AND AGE:

BREED:

MEALTIMES:

FOOD AND WATER:

TREATS:

FAVORITE TOYS:

NOTES AND INSTRUCTIONS

NAME AND AGE:

BREED:

MEALTIMES:

FOOD AND WATER:

TREATS:

FAVORITE TOYS:

NOTES AND INSTRUCTIONS

NAME AND AGE:

BREED:

MEALTIMES:

FOOD AND WATER:

TREATS:

FAVORITE TOYS:

NOTES AND INSTRUCTIONS

NAME AND AGE:

BREED:

MEALTIMES:

FOOD AND WATER:

TREATS:

FAVORITE TOYS:

NOTES AND INSTRUCTIONS

HOUSE SITTING GUIDE PET INFORMATION

VET INFORMATION	
NAME:	PHONE:
ADDRESS:	
ROUTE:	

NAME AND AGE:

BREED:

MEALTIMES:

FOOD AND WATER:

TREATS:

FAVORITE TOYS:

NOTES AND INSTRUCTIONS

NAME AND AGE:

BREED:

MEALTIMES:

FOOD AND WATER:

TREATS:

FAVORITE TOYS:

NOTES AND INSTRUCTIONS

NAME AND AGE:

BREED:

MEALTIMES:

FOOD AND WATER:

TREATS:

FAVORITE TOYS:

NOTES AND INSTRUCTIONS

NAME AND AGE:

BREED:

MEALTIMES:

FOOD AND WATER:

TREATS:

FAVORITE TOYS:

NOTES AND INSTRUCTIONS

HOUSE SITTING GUIDE PET INFORMATION

VET INFORMATION

NAME: PHONE:

ADDRESS:

ROUTE:

NAME AND AGE:

BREED:

MEALTIMES:

FOOD AND WATER:

TREATS:

FAVORITE TOYS:

NOTES AND INSTRUCTIONS

NAME AND AGE:

BREED:

MEALTIMES:

FOOD AND WATER:

TREATS:

FAVORITE TOYS:

NOTES AND INSTRUCTIONS

NAME AND AGE:

BREED:

MEALTIMES:

FOOD AND WATER:

TREATS:

FAVORITE TOYS:

NOTES AND INSTRUCTIONS

NAME AND AGE:

BREED:

MEALTIMES:

FOOD AND WATER:

TREATS:

FAVORITE TOYS:

NOTES AND INSTRUCTIONS

HOUSE SITTING GUIDE PET INFORMATION

VET INFORMATION

NAME: PHONE:

ADDRESS:

ROUTE:

NAME AND AGE:

BREED:

MEALTIMES:

FOOD AND WATER:

TREATS:

FAVORITE TOYS:

NOTES AND INSTRUCTIONS

NAME AND AGE:

BREED:

MEALTIMES:

FOOD AND WATER:

TREATS:

FAVORITE TOYS:

NOTES AND INSTRUCTIONS

NAME AND AGE:

BREED:

MEALTIMES:

FOOD AND WATER:

TREATS:

FAVORITE TOYS:

NOTES AND INSTRUCTIONS

NAME AND AGE:

BREED:

MEALTIMES:

FOOD AND WATER:

TREATS:

FAVORITE TOYS:

NOTES AND INSTRUCTIONS

HOUSE SITTING GUIDE PET INFORMATION

VET INFORMATION

NAME: PHONE:

ADDRESS:

ROUTE:

NAME AND AGE:

BREED:

MEALTIMES:

FOOD AND WATER:

TREATS:

FAVORITE TOYS:

NOTES AND INSTRUCTIONS

NAME AND AGE:

BREED:

MEALTIMES:

FOOD AND WATER:

TREATS:

FAVORITE TOYS:

NOTES AND INSTRUCTIONS

NAME AND AGE:

BREED:

MEALTIMES:

FOOD AND WATER:

TREATS:

FAVORITE TOYS:

NOTES AND INSTRUCTIONS

NAME AND AGE:

BREED:

MEALTIMES:

FOOD AND WATER:

TREATS:

FAVORITE TOYS:

NOTES AND INSTRUCTIONS

HOUSE SITTING GUIDE PET INFORMATION

VET INFORMATION

NAME: PHONE:

ADDRESS:

ROUTE:

NAME AND AGE:

BREED:

MEALTIMES:

FOOD AND WATER:

TREATS:

FAVORITE TOYS:

NOTES AND INSTRUCTIONS

NAME AND AGE:

BREED:

MEALTIMES:

FOOD AND WATER:

TREATS:

FAVORITE TOYS:

NOTES AND INSTRUCTIONS

NAME AND AGE:

BREED:

MEALTIMES:

FOOD AND WATER:

TREATS:

FAVORITE TOYS:

NOTES AND INSTRUCTIONS

NAME AND AGE:

BREED:

MEALTIMES:

FOOD AND WATER:

TREATS:

FAVORITE TOYS:

NOTES AND INSTRUCTIONS

HOUSE SITTING GUIDE PET INFORMATION

VET INFORMATION

NAME: PHONE:

ADDRESS:

ROUTE:

NAME AND AGE:

BREED:

MEALTIMES:

FOOD AND WATER:

TREATS:

FAVORITE TOYS:

NOTES AND INSTRUCTIONS

NAME AND AGE:

BREED:

MEALTIMES:

FOOD AND WATER:

TREATS:

FAVORITE TOYS:

NOTES AND INSTRUCTIONS

NAME AND AGE:

BREED:

MEALTIMES:

FOOD AND WATER:

TREATS:

FAVORITE TOYS:

NOTES AND INSTRUCTIONS

NAME AND AGE:

BREED:

MEALTIMES:

FOOD AND WATER:

TREATS:

FAVORITE TOYS:

NOTES AND INSTRUCTIONS

HOUSE SITTING GUIDE PET INFORMATION

VET INFORMATION

NAME: PHONE:

ADDRESS:

ROUTE:

NAME AND AGE:

BREED:

MEALTIMES:

FOOD AND WATER:

TREATS:

FAVORITE TOYS:

NOTES AND INSTRUCTIONS

NAME AND AGE:

BREED:

MEALTIMES:

FOOD AND WATER:

TREATS:

FAVORITE TOYS:

NOTES AND INSTRUCTIONS

NAME AND AGE:

BREED:

MEALTIMES:

FOOD AND WATER:

TREATS:

FAVORITE TOYS:

NOTES AND INSTRUCTIONS

NAME AND AGE:

BREED:

MEALTIMES:

FOOD AND WATER:

TREATS:

FAVORITE TOYS:

NOTES AND INSTRUCTIONS

HOUSE SITTING GUIDE PET INFORMATION

VET INFORMATION

NAME: PHONE:

ADDRESS:

ROUTE:

NAME AND AGE:

BREED:

MEALTIMES:

FOOD AND WATER:

TREATS:

FAVORITE TOYS:

NOTES AND INSTRUCTIONS

NAME AND AGE:

BREED:

MEALTIMES:

FOOD AND WATER:

TREATS:

FAVORITE TOYS:

NOTES AND INSTRUCTIONS

NAME AND AGE:

BREED:

MEALTIMES:

FOOD AND WATER:

TREATS:

FAVORITE TOYS:

NOTES AND INSTRUCTIONS

NAME AND AGE:

BREED:

MEALTIMES:

FOOD AND WATER:

TREATS:

FAVORITE TOYS:

NOTES AND INSTRUCTIONS

HOUSE SITTING GUIDE PET INFORMATION

VET INFORMATION

NAME: PHONE:

ADDRESS:

ROUTE:

NAME AND AGE:

BREED:

MEALTIMES:

FOOD AND WATER:

TREATS:

FAVORITE TOYS:

NOTES AND INSTRUCTIONS

NAME AND AGE:

BREED:

MEALTIMES:

FOOD AND WATER:

TREATS:

FAVORITE TOYS:

NOTES AND INSTRUCTIONS

NAME AND AGE:

BREED:

MEALTIMES:

FOOD AND WATER:

TREATS:

FAVORITE TOYS:

NOTES AND INSTRUCTIONS

NAME AND AGE:

BREED:

MEALTIMES:

FOOD AND WATER:

TREATS:

FAVORITE TOYS:

NOTES AND INSTRUCTIONS

HOUSE SITTING GUIDE PET INFORMATION

VET INFORMATION

NAME: PHONE:

ADDRESS:

ROUTE:

NAME AND AGE:

BREED:

MEALTIMES:

FOOD AND WATER:

TREATS:

FAVORITE TOYS:

NOTES AND INSTRUCTIONS

NAME AND AGE:

BREED:

MEALTIMES:

FOOD AND WATER:

TREATS:

FAVORITE TOYS:

NOTES AND INSTRUCTIONS

NAME AND AGE:

BREED:

MEALTIMES:

FOOD AND WATER:

TREATS:

FAVORITE TOYS:

NOTES AND INSTRUCTIONS

NAME AND AGE:

BREED:

MEALTIMES:

FOOD AND WATER:

TREATS:

FAVORITE TOYS:

NOTES AND INSTRUCTIONS

HOUSE SITTING GUIDE PET INFORMATION

VET INFORMATION

NAME: PHONE:

ADDRESS:

ROUTE:

NAME AND AGE:

BREED:

MEALTIMES:

FOOD AND WATER:

TREATS:

FAVORITE TOYS:

NOTES AND INSTRUCTIONS

NAME AND AGE:

BREED:

MEALTIMES:

FOOD AND WATER:

TREATS:

FAVORITE TOYS:

NOTES AND INSTRUCTIONS

NAME AND AGE:

BREED:

MEALTIMES:

FOOD AND WATER:

TREATS:

FAVORITE TOYS:

NOTES AND INSTRUCTIONS

NAME AND AGE:

BREED:

MEALTIMES:

FOOD AND WATER:

TREATS:

FAVORITE TOYS:

NOTES AND INSTRUCTIONS

HOUSE SITTING GUIDE PET INFORMATION

VET INFORMATION

NAME: PHONE:

ADDRESS:

ROUTE:

NAME AND AGE:

BREED:

MEALTIMES:

FOOD AND WATER:

TREATS:

FAVORITE TOYS:

NOTES AND INSTRUCTIONS

NAME AND AGE:

BREED:

MEALTIMES:

FOOD AND WATER:

TREATS:

FAVORITE TOYS:

NOTES AND INSTRUCTIONS

NAME AND AGE:

BREED:

MEALTIMES:

FOOD AND WATER:

TREATS:

FAVORITE TOYS:

NOTES AND INSTRUCTIONS

NAME AND AGE:

BREED:

MEALTIMES:

FOOD AND WATER:

TREATS:

FAVORITE TOYS:

NOTES AND INSTRUCTIONS

HOUSE SITTING GUIDE PET INFORMATION

VET INFORMATION	
NAME:	PHONE:
ADDRESS:	
ROUTE:	

NAME AND AGE:
BREED:
MEALTIMES:
FOOD AND WATER:
TREATS:
FAVORITE TOYS:
NOTES AND INSTRUCTIONS

NAME AND AGE:
BREED:
MEALTIMES:
FOOD AND WATER:
TREATS:
FAVORITE TOYS:
NOTES AND INSTRUCTIONS

NAME AND AGE:
BREED:
MEALTIMES:
FOOD AND WATER:
TREATS:
FAVORITE TOYS:
NOTES AND INSTRUCTIONS

NAME AND AGE:
BREED:
MEALTIMES:
FOOD AND WATER:
TREATS:
FAVORITE TOYS:
NOTES AND INSTRUCTIONS

HOUSE SITTING GUIDE PET INFORMATION

VET INFORMATION

NAME: PHONE:

ADDRESS:

ROUTE:

NAME AND AGE:

BREED:

MEALTIMES:

FOOD AND WATER:

TREATS:

FAVORITE TOYS:

NOTES AND INSTRUCTIONS

NAME AND AGE:

BREED:

MEALTIMES:

FOOD AND WATER:

TREATS:

FAVORITE TOYS:

NOTES AND INSTRUCTIONS

NAME AND AGE:

BREED:

MEALTIMES:

FOOD AND WATER:

TREATS:

FAVORITE TOYS:

NOTES AND INSTRUCTIONS

NAME AND AGE:

BREED:

MEALTIMES:

FOOD AND WATER:

TREATS:

FAVORITE TOYS:

NOTES AND INSTRUCTIONS

HOUSE SITTING GUIDE PET INFORMATION

VET INFORMATION

NAME: PHONE:

ADDRESS:

ROUTE:

NAME AND AGE:

BREED:

MEALTIMES:

FOOD AND WATER:

TREATS:

FAVORITE TOYS:

NOTES AND INSTRUCTIONS

NAME AND AGE:

BREED:

MEALTIMES:

FOOD AND WATER:

TREATS:

FAVORITE TOYS:

NOTES AND INSTRUCTIONS

NAME AND AGE:

BREED:

MEALTIMES:

FOOD AND WATER:

TREATS:

FAVORITE TOYS:

NOTES AND INSTRUCTIONS

NAME AND AGE:

BREED:

MEALTIMES:

FOOD AND WATER:

TREATS:

FAVORITE TOYS:

NOTES AND INSTRUCTIONS

HOUSE SITTING GUIDE PET INFORMATION

VET INFORMATION

NAME: PHONE:

ADDRESS:

ROUTE:

NAME AND AGE:

BREED:

MEALTIMES:

FOOD AND WATER:

TREATS:

FAVORITE TOYS:

NOTES AND INSTRUCTIONS

NAME AND AGE:

BREED:

MEALTIMES:

FOOD AND WATER:

TREATS:

FAVORITE TOYS:

NOTES AND INSTRUCTIONS

NAME AND AGE:

BREED:

MEALTIMES:

FOOD AND WATER:

TREATS:

FAVORITE TOYS:

NOTES AND INSTRUCTIONS

NAME AND AGE:

BREED:

MEALTIMES:

FOOD AND WATER:

TREATS:

FAVORITE TOYS:

NOTES AND INSTRUCTIONS

HOUSE SITTING GUIDE PET INFORMATION

VET INFORMATION

NAME: PHONE:

ADDRESS:

ROUTE:

NAME AND AGE:

BREED:

MEALTIMES:

FOOD AND WATER:

TREATS:

FAVORITE TOYS:

NOTES AND INSTRUCTIONS

NAME AND AGE:

BREED:

MEALTIMES:

FOOD AND WATER:

TREATS:

FAVORITE TOYS:

NOTES AND INSTRUCTIONS

NAME AND AGE:

BREED:

MEALTIMES:

FOOD AND WATER:

TREATS:

FAVORITE TOYS:

NOTES AND INSTRUCTIONS

NAME AND AGE:

BREED:

MEALTIMES:

FOOD AND WATER:

TREATS:

FAVORITE TOYS:

NOTES AND INSTRUCTIONS

HOUSE SITTING GUIDE PET INFORMATION

VET INFORMATION

NAME: PHONE:

ADDRESS:

ROUTE:

NAME AND AGE:

BREED:

MEALTIMES:

FOOD AND WATER:

TREATS:

FAVORITE TOYS:

NOTES AND INSTRUCTIONS

NAME AND AGE:

BREED:

MEALTIMES:

FOOD AND WATER:

TREATS:

FAVORITE TOYS:

NOTES AND INSTRUCTIONS

NAME AND AGE:

BREED:

MEALTIMES:

FOOD AND WATER:

TREATS:

FAVORITE TOYS:

NOTES AND INSTRUCTIONS

NAME AND AGE:

BREED:

MEALTIMES:

FOOD AND WATER:

TREATS:

FAVORITE TOYS:

NOTES AND INSTRUCTIONS

HOUSE SITTING GUIDE PET INFORMATION

VET INFORMATION

NAME: PHONE:

ADDRESS:

ROUTE:

NAME AND AGE:

BREED:

MEALTIMES:

FOOD AND WATER:

TREATS:

FAVORITE TOYS:

NOTES AND INSTRUCTIONS

NAME AND AGE:

BREED:

MEALTIMES:

FOOD AND WATER:

TREATS:

FAVORITE TOYS:

NOTES AND INSTRUCTIONS

NAME AND AGE:

BREED:

MEALTIMES:

FOOD AND WATER:

TREATS:

FAVORITE TOYS:

NOTES AND INSTRUCTIONS

NAME AND AGE:

BREED:

MEALTIMES:

FOOD AND WATER:

TREATS:

FAVORITE TOYS:

NOTES AND INSTRUCTIONS

HOUSE SITTING GUIDE PET INFORMATION

VET INFORMATION

NAME: PHONE:

ADDRESS:

ROUTE:

NAME AND AGE:

BREED:

MEALTIMES:

FOOD AND WATER:

TREATS:

FAVORITE TOYS:

NOTES AND INSTRUCTIONS

NAME AND AGE:

BREED:

MEALTIMES:

FOOD AND WATER:

TREATS:

FAVORITE TOYS:

NOTES AND INSTRUCTIONS

NAME AND AGE:

BREED:

MEALTIMES:

FOOD AND WATER:

TREATS:

FAVORITE TOYS:

NOTES AND INSTRUCTIONS

NAME AND AGE:

BREED:

MEALTIMES:

FOOD AND WATER:

TREATS:

FAVORITE TOYS:

NOTES AND INSTRUCTIONS

HOUSE SITTING GUIDE PET INFORMATION

VET INFORMATION

NAME: PHONE:

ADDRESS:

ROUTE:

NAME AND AGE:

BREED:

MEALTIMES:

FOOD AND WATER:

TREATS:

FAVORITE TOYS:

NOTES AND INSTRUCTIONS

NAME AND AGE:

BREED:

MEALTIMES:

FOOD AND WATER:

TREATS:

FAVORITE TOYS:

NOTES AND INSTRUCTIONS

NAME AND AGE:

BREED:

MEALTIMES:

FOOD AND WATER:

TREATS:

FAVORITE TOYS:

NOTES AND INSTRUCTIONS

NAME AND AGE:

BREED:

MEALTIMES:

FOOD AND WATER:

TREATS:

FAVORITE TOYS:

NOTES AND INSTRUCTIONS

HOUSE SITTING GUIDE PET INFORMATION

VET INFORMATION

NAME: PHONE:

ADDRESS:

ROUTE:

NAME AND AGE:

BREED:

MEALTIMES:

FOOD AND WATER:

TREATS:

FAVORITE TOYS:

NOTES AND INSTRUCTIONS

NAME AND AGE:

BREED:

MEALTIMES:

FOOD AND WATER:

TREATS:

FAVORITE TOYS:

NOTES AND INSTRUCTIONS

NAME AND AGE:

BREED:

MEALTIMES:

FOOD AND WATER:

TREATS:

FAVORITE TOYS:

NOTES AND INSTRUCTIONS

NAME AND AGE:

BREED:

MEALTIMES:

FOOD AND WATER:

TREATS:

FAVORITE TOYS:

NOTES AND INSTRUCTIONS

HOUSE SITTING GUIDE PET INFORMATION

VET INFORMATION

NAME: PHONE:

ADDRESS:

ROUTE:

NAME AND AGE:

BREED:

MEALTIMES:

FOOD AND WATER:

TREATS:

FAVORITE TOYS:

NOTES AND INSTRUCTIONS

NAME AND AGE:

BREED:

MEALTIMES:

FOOD AND WATER:

TREATS:

FAVORITE TOYS:

NOTES AND INSTRUCTIONS

NAME AND AGE:

BREED:

MEALTIMES:

FOOD AND WATER:

TREATS:

FAVORITE TOYS:

NOTES AND INSTRUCTIONS

NAME AND AGE:

BREED:

MEALTIMES:

FOOD AND WATER:

TREATS:

FAVORITE TOYS:

NOTES AND INSTRUCTIONS

HOUSE SITTING GUIDE PET INFORMATION

VET INFORMATION

NAME: PHONE:

ADDRESS:

ROUTE:

NAME AND AGE:

BREED:

MEALTIMES:

FOOD AND WATER:

TREATS:

FAVORITE TOYS:

NOTES AND INSTRUCTIONS

NAME AND AGE:

BREED:

MEALTIMES:

FOOD AND WATER:

TREATS:

FAVORITE TOYS:

NOTES AND INSTRUCTIONS

NAME AND AGE:

BREED:

MEALTIMES:

FOOD AND WATER:

TREATS:

FAVORITE TOYS:

NOTES AND INSTRUCTIONS

NAME AND AGE:

BREED:

MEALTIMES:

FOOD AND WATER:

TREATS:

FAVORITE TOYS:

NOTES AND INSTRUCTIONS

HOUSE SITTING GUIDE PET INFORMATION

VET INFORMATION	
NAME:	PHONE:
ADDRESS:	
ROUTE:	

NAME AND AGE:
BREED:
MEALTIMES:
FOOD AND WATER:
TREATS:
FAVORITE TOYS:
NOTES AND INSTRUCTIONS

NAME AND AGE:
BREED:
MEALTIMES:
FOOD AND WATER:
TREATS:
FAVORITE TOYS:
NOTES AND INSTRUCTIONS

NAME AND AGE:
BREED:
MEALTIMES:
FOOD AND WATER:
TREATS:
FAVORITE TOYS:
NOTES AND INSTRUCTIONS

NAME AND AGE:
BREED:
MEALTIMES:
FOOD AND WATER:
TREATS:
FAVORITE TOYS:
NOTES AND INSTRUCTIONS

HOUSE SITTING GUIDE PET INFORMATION

VET INFORMATION

NAME: PHONE:

ADDRESS:

ROUTE:

NAME AND AGE:

BREED:

MEALTIMES:

FOOD AND WATER:

TREATS:

FAVORITE TOYS:

NOTES AND INSTRUCTIONS

NAME AND AGE:

BREED:

MEALTIMES:

FOOD AND WATER:

TREATS:

FAVORITE TOYS:

NOTES AND INSTRUCTIONS

NAME AND AGE:

BREED:

MEALTIMES:

FOOD AND WATER:

TREATS:

FAVORITE TOYS:

NOTES AND INSTRUCTIONS

NAME AND AGE:

BREED:

MEALTIMES:

FOOD AND WATER:

TREATS:

FAVORITE TOYS:

NOTES AND INSTRUCTIONS

HOUSE SITTING GUIDE PET INFORMATION

VET INFORMATION

NAME: PHONE:

ADDRESS:

ROUTE:

NAME AND AGE:

BREED:

MEALTIMES:

FOOD AND WATER:

TREATS:

FAVORITE TOYS:

NOTES AND INSTRUCTIONS

NAME AND AGE:

BREED:

MEALTIMES:

FOOD AND WATER:

TREATS:

FAVORITE TOYS:

NOTES AND INSTRUCTIONS

NAME AND AGE:

BREED:

MEALTIMES:

FOOD AND WATER:

TREATS:

FAVORITE TOYS:

NOTES AND INSTRUCTIONS

NAME AND AGE:

BREED:

MEALTIMES:

FOOD AND WATER:

TREATS:

FAVORITE TOYS:

NOTES AND INSTRUCTIONS

HOUSE SITTING GUIDE PET INFORMATION

VET INFORMATION	
NAME:	PHONE:
ADDRESS:	
ROUTE:	

NAME AND AGE:

BREED:

MEALTIMES:

FOOD AND WATER:

TREATS:

FAVORITE TOYS:

NOTES AND INSTRUCTIONS

NAME AND AGE:

BREED:

MEALTIMES:

FOOD AND WATER:

TREATS:

FAVORITE TOYS:

NOTES AND INSTRUCTIONS

NAME AND AGE:

BREED:

MEALTIMES:

FOOD AND WATER:

TREATS:

FAVORITE TOYS:

NOTES AND INSTRUCTIONS

NAME AND AGE:

BREED:

MEALTIMES:

FOOD AND WATER:

TREATS:

FAVORITE TOYS:

NOTES AND INSTRUCTIONS

HOUSE SITTING GUIDE PET INFORMATION

VET INFORMATION

NAME: PHONE:

ADDRESS:

ROUTE:

NAME AND AGE:

BREED:

MEALTIMES:

FOOD AND WATER:

TREATS:

FAVORITE TOYS:

NOTES AND INSTRUCTIONS

NAME AND AGE:

BREED:

MEALTIMES:

FOOD AND WATER:

TREATS:

FAVORITE TOYS:

NOTES AND INSTRUCTIONS

NAME AND AGE:

BREED:

MEALTIMES:

FOOD AND WATER:

TREATS:

FAVORITE TOYS:

NOTES AND INSTRUCTIONS

NAME AND AGE:

BREED:

MEALTIMES:

FOOD AND WATER:

TREATS:

FAVORITE TOYS:

NOTES AND INSTRUCTIONS

HOUSE SITTING GUIDE PET INFORMATION

VET INFORMATION

NAME: PHONE:

ADDRESS:

ROUTE:

NAME AND AGE:

BREED:

MEALTIMES:

FOOD AND WATER:

TREATS:

FAVORITE TOYS:

NOTES AND INSTRUCTIONS

NAME AND AGE:

BREED:

MEALTIMES:

FOOD AND WATER:

TREATS:

FAVORITE TOYS:

NOTES AND INSTRUCTIONS

NAME AND AGE:

BREED:

MEALTIMES:

FOOD AND WATER:

TREATS:

FAVORITE TOYS:

NOTES AND INSTRUCTIONS

NAME AND AGE:

BREED:

MEALTIMES:

FOOD AND WATER:

TREATS:

FAVORITE TOYS:

NOTES AND INSTRUCTIONS

HOUSE SITTING GUIDE PET INFORMATION

VET INFORMATION	
NAME:	PHONE:
ADDRESS:	
ROUTE:	

NAME AND AGE:
BREED:
MEALTIMES:
FOOD AND WATER:
TREATS:
FAVORITE TOYS:
NOTES AND INSTRUCTIONS

NAME AND AGE:
BREED:
MEALTIMES:
FOOD AND WATER:
TREATS:
FAVORITE TOYS:
NOTES AND INSTRUCTIONS

NAME AND AGE:
BREED:
MEALTIMES:
FOOD AND WATER:
TREATS:
FAVORITE TOYS:
NOTES AND INSTRUCTIONS

NAME AND AGE:
BREED:
MEALTIMES:
FOOD AND WATER:
TREATS:
FAVORITE TOYS:
NOTES AND INSTRUCTIONS

HOUSE SITTING GUIDE PET INFORMATION

VET INFORMATION	
NAME:	PHONE:
ADDRESS:	
ROUTE:	

NAME AND AGE:
BREED:
MEALTIMES:
FOOD AND WATER:
TREATS:
FAVORITE TOYS:
NOTES AND INSTRUCTIONS

NAME AND AGE:
BREED:
MEALTIMES:
FOOD AND WATER:
TREATS:
FAVORITE TOYS:
NOTES AND INSTRUCTIONS

NAME AND AGE:
BREED:
MEALTIMES:
FOOD AND WATER:
TREATS:
FAVORITE TOYS:
NOTES AND INSTRUCTIONS

NAME AND AGE:
BREED:
MEALTIMES:
FOOD AND WATER:
TREATS:
FAVORITE TOYS:
NOTES AND INSTRUCTIONS

HOUSE SITTING GUIDE PET INFORMATION

VET INFORMATION	
NAME:	PHONE:
ADDRESS:	
ROUTE:	

NAME AND AGE:
BREED:
MEALTIMES:
FOOD AND WATER:
TREATS:
FAVORITE TOYS:
NOTES AND INSTRUCTIONS

NAME AND AGE:
BREED:
MEALTIMES:
FOOD AND WATER:
TREATS:
FAVORITE TOYS:
NOTES AND INSTRUCTIONS

NAME AND AGE:
BREED:
MEALTIMES:
FOOD AND WATER:
TREATS:
FAVORITE TOYS:
NOTES AND INSTRUCTIONS

NAME AND AGE:
BREED:
MEALTIMES:
FOOD AND WATER:
TREATS:
FAVORITE TOYS:
NOTES AND INSTRUCTIONS

HOUSE SITTING GUIDE PET INFORMATION

VET INFORMATION

NAME: PHONE:

ADDRESS:

ROUTE:

NAME AND AGE:

BREED:

MEALTIMES:

FOOD AND WATER:

TREATS:

FAVORITE TOYS:

NOTES AND INSTRUCTIONS

NAME AND AGE:

BREED:

MEALTIMES:

FOOD AND WATER:

TREATS:

FAVORITE TOYS:

NOTES AND INSTRUCTIONS

NAME AND AGE:

BREED:

MEALTIMES:

FOOD AND WATER:

TREATS:

FAVORITE TOYS:

NOTES AND INSTRUCTIONS

NAME AND AGE:

BREED:

MEALTIMES:

FOOD AND WATER:

TREATS:

FAVORITE TOYS:

NOTES AND INSTRUCTIONS

HOUSE SITTING GUIDE PET INFORMATION

VET INFORMATION

NAME: PHONE:

ADDRESS:

ROUTE:

NAME AND AGE:

BREED:

MEALTIMES:

FOOD AND WATER:

TREATS:

FAVORITE TOYS:

NOTES AND INSTRUCTIONS

NAME AND AGE:

BREED:

MEALTIMES:

FOOD AND WATER:

TREATS:

FAVORITE TOYS:

NOTES AND INSTRUCTIONS

NAME AND AGE:

BREED:

MEALTIMES:

FOOD AND WATER:

TREATS:

FAVORITE TOYS:

NOTES AND INSTRUCTIONS

NAME AND AGE:

BREED:

MEALTIMES:

FOOD AND WATER:

TREATS:

FAVORITE TOYS:

NOTES AND INSTRUCTIONS

HOUSE SITTING GUIDE PET INFORMATION

VET INFORMATION

NAME: PHONE:

ADDRESS:

ROUTE:

NAME AND AGE:

BREED:

MEALTIMES:

FOOD AND WATER:

TREATS:

FAVORITE TOYS:

NOTES AND INSTRUCTIONS

NAME AND AGE:

BREED:

MEALTIMES:

FOOD AND WATER:

TREATS:

FAVORITE TOYS:

NOTES AND INSTRUCTIONS

NAME AND AGE:

BREED:

MEALTIMES:

FOOD AND WATER:

TREATS:

FAVORITE TOYS:

NOTES AND INSTRUCTIONS

NAME AND AGE:

BREED:

MEALTIMES:

FOOD AND WATER:

TREATS:

FAVORITE TOYS:

NOTES AND INSTRUCTIONS

HOUSE SITTING GUIDE PET INFORMATION

VET INFORMATION	
NAME:	PHONE:
ADDRESS:	
ROUTE:	

NAME AND AGE:
BREED:
MEALTIMES:
FOOD AND WATER:
TREATS:
FAVORITE TOYS:
NOTES AND INSTRUCTIONS

NAME AND AGE:
BREED:
MEALTIMES:
FOOD AND WATER:
TREATS:
FAVORITE TOYS:
NOTES AND INSTRUCTIONS

NAME AND AGE:
BREED:
MEALTIMES:
FOOD AND WATER:
TREATS:
FAVORITE TOYS:
NOTES AND INSTRUCTIONS

NAME AND AGE:
BREED:
MEALTIMES:
FOOD AND WATER:
TREATS:
FAVORITE TOYS:
NOTES AND INSTRUCTIONS

HOUSE SITTING GUIDE PET INFORMATION

VET INFORMATION

NAME: PHONE:

ADDRESS:

ROUTE:

NAME AND AGE:

BREED:

MEALTIMES:

FOOD AND WATER:

TREATS:

FAVORITE TOYS:

NOTES AND INSTRUCTIONS

NAME AND AGE:

BREED:

MEALTIMES:

FOOD AND WATER:

TREATS:

FAVORITE TOYS:

NOTES AND INSTRUCTIONS

NAME AND AGE:

BREED:

MEALTIMES:

FOOD AND WATER:

TREATS:

FAVORITE TOYS:

NOTES AND INSTRUCTIONS

NAME AND AGE:

BREED:

MEALTIMES:

FOOD AND WATER:

TREATS:

FAVORITE TOYS:

NOTES AND INSTRUCTIONS

HOUSE SITTING GUIDE PET INFORMATION

VET INFORMATION	
NAME:	PHONE:
ADDRESS:	
ROUTE:	

NAME AND AGE:
BREED:
MEALTIMES:
FOOD AND WATER:
TREATS:
FAVORITE TOYS:
NOTES AND INSTRUCTIONS

NAME AND AGE:
BREED:
MEALTIMES:
FOOD AND WATER:
TREATS:
FAVORITE TOYS:
NOTES AND INSTRUCTIONS

NAME AND AGE:
BREED:
MEALTIMES:
FOOD AND WATER:
TREATS:
FAVORITE TOYS:
NOTES AND INSTRUCTIONS

NAME AND AGE:
BREED:
MEALTIMES:
FOOD AND WATER:
TREATS:
FAVORITE TOYS:
NOTES AND INSTRUCTIONS

HOUSE SITTING GUIDE PET INFORMATION

VET INFORMATION

NAME: PHONE:

ADDRESS:

ROUTE:

NAME AND AGE:

BREED:

MEALTIMES:

FOOD AND WATER:

TREATS:

FAVORITE TOYS:

NOTES AND INSTRUCTIONS

NAME AND AGE:

BREED:

MEALTIMES:

FOOD AND WATER:

TREATS:

FAVORITE TOYS:

NOTES AND INSTRUCTIONS

NAME AND AGE:

BREED:

MEALTIMES:

FOOD AND WATER:

TREATS:

FAVORITE TOYS:

NOTES AND INSTRUCTIONS

NAME AND AGE:

BREED:

MEALTIMES:

FOOD AND WATER:

TREATS:

FAVORITE TOYS:

NOTES AND INSTRUCTIONS

HOUSE SITTING GUIDE PET INFORMATION

VET INFORMATION

NAME: PHONE:

ADDRESS:

ROUTE:

NAME AND AGE:

BREED:

MEALTIMES:

FOOD AND WATER:

TREATS:

FAVORITE TOYS:

NOTES AND INSTRUCTIONS

NAME AND AGE:

BREED:

MEALTIMES:

FOOD AND WATER:

TREATS:

FAVORITE TOYS:

NOTES AND INSTRUCTIONS

NAME AND AGE:

BREED:

MEALTIMES:

FOOD AND WATER:

TREATS:

FAVORITE TOYS:

NOTES AND INSTRUCTIONS

NAME AND AGE:

BREED:

MEALTIMES:

FOOD AND WATER:

TREATS:

FAVORITE TOYS:

NOTES AND INSTRUCTIONS

HOUSE SITTING GUIDE PET INFORMATION

VET INFORMATION

NAME: _____ PHONE: _____

ADDRESS: _____

ROUTE:

NAME AND AGE:

BREED:

MEALTIMES:

FOOD AND WATER:

TREATS:

FAVORITE TOYS:

NOTES AND INSTRUCTIONS

NAME AND AGE:

BREED:

MEALTIMES:

FOOD AND WATER:

TREATS:

FAVORITE TOYS:

NOTES AND INSTRUCTIONS

NAME AND AGE:

BREED:

MEALTIMES:

FOOD AND WATER:

TREATS:

FAVORITE TOYS:

NOTES AND INSTRUCTIONS

NAME AND AGE:

BREED:

MEALTIMES:

FOOD AND WATER:

TREATS:

FAVORITE TOYS:

NOTES AND INSTRUCTIONS

HOUSE SITTING GUIDE PET INFORMATION

VET INFORMATION

NAME: PHONE:

ADDRESS:

ROUTE:

NAME AND AGE:

BREED:

MEALTIMES:

FOOD AND WATER:

TREATS:

FAVORITE TOYS:

NOTES AND INSTRUCTIONS

NAME AND AGE:

BREED:

MEALTIMES:

FOOD AND WATER:

TREATS:

FAVORITE TOYS:

NOTES AND INSTRUCTIONS

NAME AND AGE:

BREED:

MEALTIMES:

FOOD AND WATER:

TREATS:

FAVORITE TOYS:

NOTES AND INSTRUCTIONS

NAME AND AGE:

BREED:

MEALTIMES:

FOOD AND WATER:

TREATS:

FAVORITE TOYS:

NOTES AND INSTRUCTIONS

HOUSE SITTING GUIDE PET INFORMATION

VET INFORMATION

NAME: PHONE:

ADDRESS:

ROUTE:

NAME AND AGE:

BREED:

MEALTIMES:

FOOD AND WATER:

TREATS:

FAVORITE TOYS:

NOTES AND INSTRUCTIONS

NAME AND AGE:

BREED:

MEALTIMES:

FOOD AND WATER:

TREATS:

FAVORITE TOYS:

NOTES AND INSTRUCTIONS

NAME AND AGE:

BREED:

MEALTIMES:

FOOD AND WATER:

TREATS:

FAVORITE TOYS:

NOTES AND INSTRUCTIONS

NAME AND AGE:

BREED:

MEALTIMES:

FOOD AND WATER:

TREATS:

FAVORITE TOYS:

NOTES AND INSTRUCTIONS

HOUSE SITTING GUIDE PET INFORMATION

VET INFORMATION	
NAME:	PHONE:
ADDRESS:	
ROUTE:	

NAME AND AGE:
BREED:
MEALTIMES:
FOOD AND WATER:
TREATS:
FAVORITE TOYS:
NOTES AND INSTRUCTIONS

NAME AND AGE:
BREED:
MEALTIMES:
FOOD AND WATER:
TREATS:
FAVORITE TOYS:
NOTES AND INSTRUCTIONS

NAME AND AGE:
BREED:
MEALTIMES:
FOOD AND WATER:
TREATS:
FAVORITE TOYS:
NOTES AND INSTRUCTIONS

NAME AND AGE:
BREED:
MEALTIMES:
FOOD AND WATER:
TREATS:
FAVORITE TOYS:
NOTES AND INSTRUCTIONS

HOUSE SITTING GUIDE PET INFORMATION

VET INFORMATION

NAME: PHONE:

ADDRESS:

ROUTE:

NAME AND AGE:

BREED:

MEALTIMES:

FOOD AND WATER:

TREATS:

FAVORITE TOYS:

NOTES AND INSTRUCTIONS

NAME AND AGE:

BREED:

MEALTIMES:

FOOD AND WATER:

TREATS:

FAVORITE TOYS:

NOTES AND INSTRUCTIONS

NAME AND AGE:

BREED:

MEALTIMES:

FOOD AND WATER:

TREATS:

FAVORITE TOYS:

NOTES AND INSTRUCTIONS

NAME AND AGE:

BREED:

MEALTIMES:

FOOD AND WATER:

TREATS:

FAVORITE TOYS:

NOTES AND INSTRUCTIONS

HOUSE SITTING GUIDE PET INFORMATION

VET INFORMATION

NAME: PHONE:

ADDRESS:

ROUTE:

NAME AND AGE:

BREED:

MEALTIMES:

FOOD AND WATER:

TREATS:

FAVORITE TOYS:

NOTES AND INSTRUCTIONS

NAME AND AGE:

BREED:

MEALTIMES:

FOOD AND WATER:

TREATS:

FAVORITE TOYS:

NOTES AND INSTRUCTIONS

NAME AND AGE:

BREED:

MEALTIMES:

FOOD AND WATER:

TREATS:

FAVORITE TOYS:

NOTES AND INSTRUCTIONS

NAME AND AGE:

BREED:

MEALTIMES:

FOOD AND WATER:

TREATS:

FAVORITE TOYS:

NOTES AND INSTRUCTIONS

HOUSE SITTING GUIDE PET INFORMATION

VET INFORMATION

NAME: PHONE:

ADDRESS:

ROUTE:

NAME AND AGE:

BREED:

MEALTIMES:

FOOD AND WATER:

TREATS:

FAVORITE TOYS:

NOTES AND INSTRUCTIONS

NAME AND AGE:

BREED:

MEALTIMES:

FOOD AND WATER:

TREATS:

FAVORITE TOYS:

NOTES AND INSTRUCTIONS

NAME AND AGE:

BREED:

MEALTIMES:

FOOD AND WATER:

TREATS:

FAVORITE TOYS:

NOTES AND INSTRUCTIONS

NAME AND AGE:

BREED:

MEALTIMES:

FOOD AND WATER:

TREATS:

FAVORITE TOYS:

NOTES AND INSTRUCTIONS

HOUSE SITTING GUIDE PET INFORMATION

VET INFORMATION	
NAME:	PHONE:
ADDRESS:	
ROUTE:	

NAME AND AGE:
BREED:
MEALTIMES:
FOOD AND WATER:
TREATS:
FAVORITE TOYS:
NOTES AND INSTRUCTIONS

NAME AND AGE:
BREED:
MEALTIMES:
FOOD AND WATER:
TREATS:
FAVORITE TOYS:
NOTES AND INSTRUCTIONS

NAME AND AGE:
BREED:
MEALTIMES:
FOOD AND WATER:
TREATS:
FAVORITE TOYS:
NOTES AND INSTRUCTIONS

NAME AND AGE:
BREED:
MEALTIMES:
FOOD AND WATER:
TREATS:
FAVORITE TOYS:
NOTES AND INSTRUCTIONS

HOUSE SITTING GUIDE PET INFORMATION

VET INFORMATION

NAME: PHONE:

ADDRESS:

ROUTE:

NAME AND AGE:

BREED:

MEALTIMES:

FOOD AND WATER:

TREATS:

FAVORITE TOYS:

NOTES AND INSTRUCTIONS

NAME AND AGE:

BREED:

MEALTIMES:

FOOD AND WATER:

TREATS:

FAVORITE TOYS:

NOTES AND INSTRUCTIONS

NAME AND AGE:

BREED:

MEALTIMES:

FOOD AND WATER:

TREATS:

FAVORITE TOYS:

NOTES AND INSTRUCTIONS

NAME AND AGE:

BREED:

MEALTIMES:

FOOD AND WATER:

TREATS:

FAVORITE TOYS:

NOTES AND INSTRUCTIONS

HOUSE SITTING GUIDE PET INFORMATION

VET INFORMATION

NAME: PHONE:

ADDRESS:

ROUTE:

NAME AND AGE:

BREED:

MEALTIMES:

FOOD AND WATER:

TREATS:

FAVORITE TOYS:

NOTES AND INSTRUCTIONS

NAME AND AGE:

BREED:

MEALTIMES:

FOOD AND WATER:

TREATS:

FAVORITE TOYS:

NOTES AND INSTRUCTIONS

NAME AND AGE:

BREED:

MEALTIMES:

FOOD AND WATER:

TREATS:

FAVORITE TOYS:

NOTES AND INSTRUCTIONS

NAME AND AGE:

BREED:

MEALTIMES:

FOOD AND WATER:

TREATS:

FAVORITE TOYS:

NOTES AND INSTRUCTIONS

HOUSE SITTING GUIDE PET INFORMATION

VET INFORMATION

NAME: PHONE:

ADDRESS:

ROUTE:

NAME AND AGE:

BREED:

MEALTIMES:

FOOD AND WATER:

TREATS:

FAVORITE TOYS:

NOTES AND INSTRUCTIONS

NAME AND AGE:

BREED:

MEALTIMES:

FOOD AND WATER:

TREATS:

FAVORITE TOYS:

NOTES AND INSTRUCTIONS

NAME AND AGE:

BREED:

MEALTIMES:

FOOD AND WATER:

TREATS:

FAVORITE TOYS:

NOTES AND INSTRUCTIONS

NAME AND AGE:

BREED:

MEALTIMES:

FOOD AND WATER:

TREATS:

FAVORITE TOYS:

NOTES AND INSTRUCTIONS

HOUSE SITTING GUIDE PET INFORMATION

VET INFORMATION

NAME: PHONE:

ADDRESS:

ROUTE:

NAME AND AGE:

BREED:

MEALTIMES:

FOOD AND WATER:

TREATS:

FAVORITE TOYS:

NOTES AND INSTRUCTIONS

NAME AND AGE:

BREED:

MEALTIMES:

FOOD AND WATER:

TREATS:

FAVORITE TOYS:

NOTES AND INSTRUCTIONS

NAME AND AGE:

BREED:

MEALTIMES:

FOOD AND WATER:

TREATS:

FAVORITE TOYS:

NOTES AND INSTRUCTIONS

NAME AND AGE:

BREED:

MEALTIMES:

FOOD AND WATER:

TREATS:

FAVORITE TOYS:

NOTES AND INSTRUCTIONS

HOUSE SITTING GUIDE PET INFORMATION

VET INFORMATION

NAME: PHONE:

ADDRESS:

ROUTE:

NAME AND AGE:

BREED:

MEALTIMES:

FOOD AND WATER:

TREATS:

FAVORITE TOYS:

NOTES AND INSTRUCTIONS

NAME AND AGE:

BREED:

MEALTIMES:

FOOD AND WATER:

TREATS:

FAVORITE TOYS:

NOTES AND INSTRUCTIONS

NAME AND AGE:

BREED:

MEALTIMES:

FOOD AND WATER:

TREATS:

FAVORITE TOYS:

NOTES AND INSTRUCTIONS

NAME AND AGE:

BREED:

MEALTIMES:

FOOD AND WATER:

TREATS:

FAVORITE TOYS:

NOTES AND INSTRUCTIONS

HOUSE SITTING GUIDE PET INFORMATION

VET INFORMATION	
NAME:	PHONE:
ADDRESS:	
ROUTE:	

NAME AND AGE:

BREED:

MEALTIMES:

FOOD AND WATER:

TREATS:

FAVORITE TOYS:

NOTES AND INSTRUCTIONS

NAME AND AGE:

BREED:

MEALTIMES:

FOOD AND WATER:

TREATS:

FAVORITE TOYS:

NOTES AND INSTRUCTIONS

NAME AND AGE:

BREED:

MEALTIMES:

FOOD AND WATER:

TREATS:

FAVORITE TOYS:

NOTES AND INSTRUCTIONS

NAME AND AGE:

BREED:

MEALTIMES:

FOOD AND WATER:

TREATS:

FAVORITE TOYS:

NOTES AND INSTRUCTIONS

HOUSE SITTING GUIDE PET INFORMATION

VET INFORMATION
NAME: PHONE:
ADDRESS:
ROUTE:

NAME AND AGE:

BREED:

MEALTIMES:

FOOD AND WATER:

TREATS:

FAVORITE TOYS:

NOTES AND INSTRUCTIONS

NAME AND AGE:

BREED:

MEALTIMES:

FOOD AND WATER:

TREATS:

FAVORITE TOYS:

NOTES AND INSTRUCTIONS

NAME AND AGE:

BREED:

MEALTIMES:

FOOD AND WATER:

TREATS:

FAVORITE TOYS:

NOTES AND INSTRUCTIONS

NAME AND AGE:

BREED:

MEALTIMES:

FOOD AND WATER:

TREATS:

FAVORITE TOYS:

NOTES AND INSTRUCTIONS

HOUSE SITTING GUIDE PET INFORMATION

VET INFORMATION	
NAME:	PHONE:
ADDRESS:	
ROUTE:	

NAME AND AGE:
BREED:
MEALTIMES:
FOOD AND WATER:
TREATS:
FAVORITE TOYS:
NOTES AND INSTRUCTIONS

NAME AND AGE:
BREED:
MEALTIMES:
FOOD AND WATER:
TREATS:
FAVORITE TOYS:
NOTES AND INSTRUCTIONS

NAME AND AGE:
BREED:
MEALTIMES:
FOOD AND WATER:
TREATS:
FAVORITE TOYS:
NOTES AND INSTRUCTIONS

NAME AND AGE:
BREED:
MEALTIMES:
FOOD AND WATER:
TREATS:
FAVORITE TOYS:
NOTES AND INSTRUCTIONS

HOUSE SITTING GUIDE PET INFORMATION

VET INFORMATION

NAME: PHONE:

ADDRESS:

ROUTE:

NAME AND AGE:

BREED:

MEALTIMES:

FOOD AND WATER:

TREATS:

FAVORITE TOYS:

NOTES AND INSTRUCTIONS

NAME AND AGE:

BREED:

MEALTIMES:

FOOD AND WATER:

TREATS:

FAVORITE TOYS:

NOTES AND INSTRUCTIONS

NAME AND AGE:

BREED:

MEALTIMES:

FOOD AND WATER:

TREATS:

FAVORITE TOYS:

NOTES AND INSTRUCTIONS

NAME AND AGE:

BREED:

MEALTIMES:

FOOD AND WATER:

TREATS:

FAVORITE TOYS:

NOTES AND INSTRUCTIONS

HOUSE SITTING GUIDE PET INFORMATION

VET INFORMATION	
NAME:	PHONE:
ADDRESS:	
ROUTE:	

NAME AND AGE:

BREED:

MEALTIMES:

FOOD AND WATER:

TREATS:

FAVORITE TOYS:

NOTES AND INSTRUCTIONS

NAME AND AGE:

BREED:

MEALTIMES:

FOOD AND WATER:

TREATS:

FAVORITE TOYS:

NOTES AND INSTRUCTIONS

NAME AND AGE:

BREED:

MEALTIMES:

FOOD AND WATER:

TREATS:

FAVORITE TOYS:

NOTES AND INSTRUCTIONS

NAME AND AGE:

BREED:

MEALTIMES:

FOOD AND WATER:

TREATS:

FAVORITE TOYS:

NOTES AND INSTRUCTIONS

HOUSE SITTING GUIDE PET INFORMATION

VET INFORMATION

NAME: PHONE:

ADDRESS:

ROUTE:

NAME AND AGE:

BREED:

MEALTIMES:

FOOD AND WATER:

TREATS:

FAVORITE TOYS:

NOTES AND INSTRUCTIONS

NAME AND AGE:

BREED:

MEALTIMES:

FOOD AND WATER:

TREATS:

FAVORITE TOYS:

NOTES AND INSTRUCTIONS

NAME AND AGE:

BREED:

MEALTIMES:

FOOD AND WATER:

TREATS:

FAVORITE TOYS:

NOTES AND INSTRUCTIONS

NAME AND AGE:

BREED:

MEALTIMES:

FOOD AND WATER:

TREATS:

FAVORITE TOYS:

NOTES AND INSTRUCTIONS

HOUSE SITTING GUIDE PET INFORMATION

VET INFORMATION	
NAME:	PHONE:
ADDRESS:	
ROUTE:	

NAME AND AGE:
BREED:
MEALTIMES:
FOOD AND WATER:
TREATS:
FAVORITE TOYS:
NOTES AND INSTRUCTIONS

NAME AND AGE:
BREED:
MEALTIMES:
FOOD AND WATER:
TREATS:
FAVORITE TOYS:
NOTES AND INSTRUCTIONS

NAME AND AGE:
BREED:
MEALTIMES:
FOOD AND WATER:
TREATS:
FAVORITE TOYS:
NOTES AND INSTRUCTIONS

NAME AND AGE:
BREED:
MEALTIMES:
FOOD AND WATER:
TREATS:
FAVORITE TOYS:
NOTES AND INSTRUCTIONS

HOUSE SITTING GUIDE PET INFORMATION

VET INFORMATION

NAME: PHONE:

ADDRESS:

ROUTE:

NAME AND AGE:

BREED:

MEALTIMES:

FOOD AND WATER:

TREATS:

FAVORITE TOYS:

NOTES AND INSTRUCTIONS

NAME AND AGE:

BREED:

MEALTIMES:

FOOD AND WATER:

TREATS:

FAVORITE TOYS:

NOTES AND INSTRUCTIONS

NAME AND AGE:

BREED:

MEALTIMES:

FOOD AND WATER:

TREATS:

FAVORITE TOYS:

NOTES AND INSTRUCTIONS

NAME AND AGE:

BREED:

MEALTIMES:

FOOD AND WATER:

TREATS:

FAVORITE TOYS:

NOTES AND INSTRUCTIONS

HOUSE SITTING GUIDE PET INFORMATION

VET INFORMATION

NAME:	PHONE:
ADDRESS:	
ROUTE:	

NAME AND AGE:

BREED:

MEALTIMES:

FOOD AND WATER:

TREATS:

FAVORITE TOYS:

NOTES AND INSTRUCTIONS

NAME AND AGE:

BREED:

MEALTIMES:

FOOD AND WATER:

TREATS:

FAVORITE TOYS:

NOTES AND INSTRUCTIONS

NAME AND AGE:

BREED:

MEALTIMES:

FOOD AND WATER:

TREATS:

FAVORITE TOYS:

NOTES AND INSTRUCTIONS

NAME AND AGE:

BREED:

MEALTIMES:

FOOD AND WATER:

TREATS:

FAVORITE TOYS:

NOTES AND INSTRUCTIONS

HOUSE SITTING GUIDE PET INFORMATION

VET INFORMATION

NAME: PHONE:

ADDRESS:

ROUTE:

NAME AND AGE:

BREED:

MEALTIMES:

FOOD AND WATER:

TREATS:

FAVORITE TOYS:

NOTES AND INSTRUCTIONS

NAME AND AGE:

BREED:

MEALTIMES:

FOOD AND WATER:

TREATS:

FAVORITE TOYS:

NOTES AND INSTRUCTIONS

NAME AND AGE:

BREED:

MEALTIMES:

FOOD AND WATER:

TREATS:

FAVORITE TOYS:

NOTES AND INSTRUCTIONS

NAME AND AGE:

BREED:

MEALTIMES:

FOOD AND WATER:

TREATS:

FAVORITE TOYS:

NOTES AND INSTRUCTIONS

HOUSE SITTING GUIDE PET INFORMATION

VET INFORMATION

NAME: PHONE:

ADDRESS:

ROUTE:

NAME AND AGE:

BREED:

MEALTIMES:

FOOD AND WATER:

TREATS:

FAVORITE TOYS:

NOTES AND INSTRUCTIONS

NAME AND AGE:

BREED:

MEALTIMES:

FOOD AND WATER:

TREATS:

FAVORITE TOYS:

NOTES AND INSTRUCTIONS

NAME AND AGE:

BREED:

MEALTIMES:

FOOD AND WATER:

TREATS:

FAVORITE TOYS:

NOTES AND INSTRUCTIONS

NAME AND AGE:

BREED:

MEALTIMES:

FOOD AND WATER:

TREATS:

FAVORITE TOYS:

NOTES AND INSTRUCTIONS

HOUSE SITTING GUIDE PET INFORMATION

VET INFORMATION

NAME: PHONE:

ADDRESS:

ROUTE:

NAME AND AGE:

BREED:

MEALTIMES:

FOOD AND WATER:

TREATS:

FAVORITE TOYS:

NOTES AND INSTRUCTIONS

NAME AND AGE:

BREED:

MEALTIMES:

FOOD AND WATER:

TREATS:

FAVORITE TOYS:

NOTES AND INSTRUCTIONS

NAME AND AGE:

BREED:

MEALTIMES:

FOOD AND WATER:

TREATS:

FAVORITE TOYS:

NOTES AND INSTRUCTIONS

NAME AND AGE:

BREED:

MEALTIMES:

FOOD AND WATER:

TREATS:

FAVORITE TOYS:

NOTES AND INSTRUCTIONS

HOUSE SITTING GUIDE PET INFORMATION

VET INFORMATION	
NAME:	PHONE:
ADDRESS:	
ROUTE:	

NAME AND AGE:
BREED:
MEALTIMES:
FOOD AND WATER:
TREATS:
FAVORITE TOYS:
NOTES AND INSTRUCTIONS

NAME AND AGE:
BREED:
MEALTIMES:
FOOD AND WATER:
TREATS:
FAVORITE TOYS:
NOTES AND INSTRUCTIONS

NAME AND AGE:
BREED:
MEALTIMES:
FOOD AND WATER:
TREATS:
FAVORITE TOYS:
NOTES AND INSTRUCTIONS

NAME AND AGE:
BREED:
MEALTIMES:
FOOD AND WATER:
TREATS:
FAVORITE TOYS:
NOTES AND INSTRUCTIONS

HOUSE SITTING GUIDE PET INFORMATION

VET INFORMATION

NAME: PHONE:

ADDRESS:

ROUTE:

NAME AND AGE:

BREED:

MEALTIMES:

FOOD AND WATER:

TREATS:

FAVORITE TOYS:

NOTES AND INSTRUCTIONS

NAME AND AGE:

BREED:

MEALTIMES:

FOOD AND WATER:

TREATS:

FAVORITE TOYS:

NOTES AND INSTRUCTIONS

NAME AND AGE:

BREED:

MEALTIMES:

FOOD AND WATER:

TREATS:

FAVORITE TOYS:

NOTES AND INSTRUCTIONS

NAME AND AGE:

BREED:

MEALTIMES:

FOOD AND WATER:

TREATS:

FAVORITE TOYS:

NOTES AND INSTRUCTIONS

HOUSE SITTING GUIDE PET INFORMATION

VET INFORMATION	
NAME:	PHONE:
ADDRESS:	
ROUTE:	

NAME AND AGE:
BREED:
MEALTIMES:
FOOD AND WATER:
TREATS:
FAVORITE TOYS:
NOTES AND INSTRUCTIONS

NAME AND AGE:
BREED:
MEALTIMES:
FOOD AND WATER:
TREATS:
FAVORITE TOYS:
NOTES AND INSTRUCTIONS

NAME AND AGE:
BREED:
MEALTIMES:
FOOD AND WATER:
TREATS:
FAVORITE TOYS:
NOTES AND INSTRUCTIONS

NAME AND AGE:
BREED:
MEALTIMES:
FOOD AND WATER:
TREATS:
FAVORITE TOYS:
NOTES AND INSTRUCTIONS

Made in the USA
Coppell, TX
01 October 2024

37978144R00056